Hello Sports Fans
"The Sports News Is On..."

Welcome fans, kids, parents, grammas and gramps.
Who will win these games and be the new champs?

Football, Baseball, Basketball, Hockey, and Soccer action.
With exciting highlights, it's a sports fan's satisfaction.

We have great teams in action, with news that's breaking.
The scores, athletes, and some highlights in the making.

Football	Baseball	Basketball	Hockey	Soccer

Wildcats - Mustangs	Eagles - Sharks	Skyhawks - Lizards	Thunderbirds - Polar Bears	Knights - Dragons

Have fun watching the action, all eyes are on the play.
And practice your reading, to surprise someone today.

Make use of those red letters and blue words, a handy guide.
All the letters have sounds, that make words, along each side.

We have the 4 building blocks of reading, shown in a chart.
Try out some of the tips, and help make the kids really smart.

Practice early reading skills using the special page format.
- see the Literacy Guide chart on page 54 -
4 Building Blocks Of Reading - With Suggested Reading Skills Activities

sportsactionbooks@gmail.com

Sports Action Kids Books - Book 1
ISBN-978-1-7771741-6-3

Copyright © Coach Craig B.Ed. 2020

The Sports News Is On !

The fans are so excited, on the edge of their seats!

The fans are riveted, each game is full of supense!

We have 5 Sports updates !

And they are nervous, no time for cell phone calls or tweets!

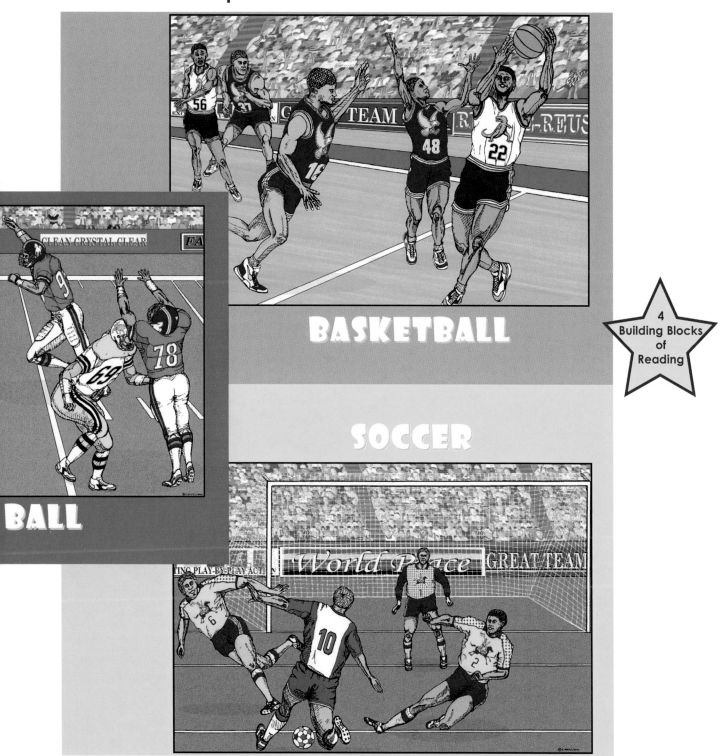

BASKETBALL

SOCCER

BALL

4 Building Blocks of Reading

Let's view the updates, all the action is so intense!

Football News Update:

The Wildcats, in yellow, white and black, are winning by four.

Wildcats

28

The Mustangs charge down field, after the high flying kick.

The Football Game Is On !

The Mustangs wearing red, white and blue, are needing to score.

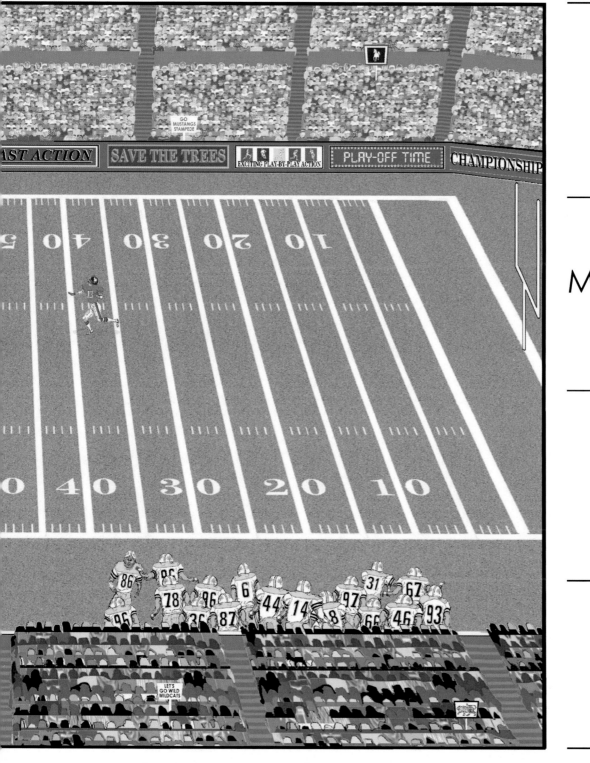

Mustangs

24

They're after the Wildcat, ready to catch the ball quick.

A a
B b
C c
D d
E e
F f
G g
H h
I i
J j
K k
L l
M m
N n
O o
P p
Q q
R r
S s
T t
U u
V v
W w
X x
Y y
Z z

© C. HICKS / 2001

He catches the football
and drives straight ahead,

catches drives the football straight and he crashing ahead into wall of red white blue

crashing into a wall of
white, blue and red.

The Wildcats have the ball, and are all set to go.

the

Wildcats

ball

have

and

all

are

set

go

across

are

Mustangs

their

linemen

row

Across are the Mustangs, their linemen in a row.

"Go Wild! Wildcats! Go!", the fans cheer up in the stands.

A a
B b
C c
D d
E e
F f
G g
H h
I i
J j
K k
L l
M m
N n
O o
P p
Q q
R r
S s
T t
U u
V v
W w
X x
Y y
Z z

The quarterback hands off the ball to his halfback.

"Go Mustangs! Stampede!",
others shout, clapping their hands.

ball

hands

off

the

quarterback

halfback

to

his

center

the

guards

fend

off

the

attack

As the center and his guards
fend off the attack.

The Wildcat turns up-field, with a deke and a feign.

Wildcats

28

OK fans! "The Football Game Is On!", who is going to win?

Now to our next sports update:

Only to be pounced on, for very little gain.

Mustangs

24

Who's cheering for the Wildcats or Mustangs, with a big grin?

Terrific baseball action !

Baseball News Update:

The Eagles in red, white and blue, play with such great skill.

Eagles

3

The Eagles are ready to play defense, and get three outs.

The Baseball Game Is On !

The Sharks wearing white, yellow and red, play with such strong will.

Sharks

4

The batter and runner are set, "play ball," the umpire shouts.

"Go! Eagles! Soar-High!", some fans cheer up in the stands.

A a
B b
C c
D d
E e
F f
G g
H h
I i
J j
K k
L l
M m
N n
O o
P p
Q q
R r
S s
T t
U u
V v
W w
X x
Y y
Z z

The pitcher checks the runner, he goes into his wind up.

"Go! Sharks-On-The-Hunt!", others shout, clapping their hands.

pitcher

the

runner

checks

goes

wind

up

into

waits

will

go

time

mind

up

make

The runner waits. Will he go?
It's time to make his mind up.

A a
B b
C c
D d
E e
F f
G g
H h
I i
J j
K k
L l
M m
N n
O o
P p
Q q
R r
S s
T t
U u
V v
W w
X x
Y y
Z z

The pitcher turns. The Shark goes! He takes off with great speed.

18

turns

pitcher

Shark

goes

off

he

takes

great

speed

steps

throw

took

good

lead

the

The pitcher steps to throw, as the Shark took a good lead.

EAGLES

3

STRIKES   BALLS

1   1

A swing and a miss! The catcher stands up, to make a throw.

swing

miss

stands

catcher

up

throw

make

he

aims

base

second

sees

runner

Shark

go

©C. HICKS/96

He aims for second base, as he sees the Shark runner go.

The Shark looks for second base, he runs, and slides for the bag.

Eagles

3

OK fans! "The Baseball Game Is On!", who is going to win?

Now to our next sports update:

The ump calls, "OUT!" The Eagle
with the ball, puts on the tag.

Sharks

4

Will you cheer for the Eagles
or the Sharks, with a big grin?

Amazing basketball action !

Basketball News Update:

The Skyhawks, in yellow, white and blue, are a really good team.

Skyhawks

90

Standing at the side-line, a Skyhawk holds the ball and waits.

The Basketball Game Is On !

The Lizards, in green, white and black, play a very smart scheme.

Lizards

90

A Lizard guards him closely, as he looks for his teammates.

A a
B b
C c
D d
E e
F f
G g
H h
I i
J j
K k
L l
M m
N n
O o
P p
Q q
R r
S s
T t
U u
V v
W w
X x
Y y
Z z

He sees a Hawk and throws
the ball, to resume the action.

26

He

Hawk

sees

and

throws

the

ball

action

resume

sprinting

catches

quick

the

with

reaction

The sprinting Hawk catches
the ball, with a quick reaction.

As the Lizard guards him, the Hawk makes an arm pump.

the

Lizard

guards

him

makes

arm

pump

looks

up

basket

then

both

them

jump

He looks up to the basket,
then both of them jump.

"Go Skyhawks! Fly-Sky-High!",
the fans cheer up in the stands.

A a
B b
C c
D d
E e
F f
G g
H h
I i
J j
K k
L l
M m
N n
O o
P p
Q q
R r
S s
T t
U u
V v
W w
X x
Y y
Z z

He shoots a jump-shot, the ball rises up and is drifting.

"Go! Lizards-Are-Wizards!",
others shout clapping their hands.

jump

shot

shoots

rises

ball

up

drifting

it

flies

net

players

move

shifting

are

and

It flies to the net, the players
move in and are shifting.

The ball bounces, with players jumping up and soaring high.

Skyhawks

90

OK fans! "The Basketball Game Is On!", who is going to win?

Now to our next sports update:

A Skyhawk taps the ball in, finishing the scoring try.

Lizards

90

Who's cheering for the Skyhawks or the Lizards, with a big grin?

Fantastic hockey action !

Hockey News Update:

The Polar Bears, in grey, white and blue, are strong and aggressive.

Thunderbirds

2

The players skate in, waiting for the puck drop, by the referee.

The Hockey Game Is On !

The Thunderbirds, in red, white and black, are fast and impressive.

Polar Bears

2

Set for the face-off, the team that scores next, earns the victory.

A a
B b
C c
D d
E e
F f
G g
H h
I i
J j
K k
L l
M m
N n
O o
P p
Q q
R r
S s
T t
U u
V v
W w
X x
Y y
Z z

© C.HICKS/96

A Thunderbird skates to the blueline, and shoots the puck in quick.

skates

Thunderbird

blueline

puck

shoots

in

quick

Polar Bear

to

check

tries

him

flies

off

stick

As a Polar Bear tries to check him,
the puck flies off his stick.

A
B
C
D
E
F
G
H
I
J
K
L
M
N
O
P
Q
R
S
T
U
V
W
X
Y
Z

a
b
c
d
e
f
g
h
i
j
k
l
m
n
o
p
q
r
s
t
u
v
w
x
y
z

A Bear makes a pass, off his hockey stick the puck slides.

Bear

pass

puck

off

hockey

stick

slides

he

aims

winger

the

ice

along

puck

glides

He aims for his winger, along
the ice the puck glides.

"Go! Make-It-Thunder! Birds!", fans cheer up in the stands.

A a
B b
C c
D d
E e
F f
G g
H h
I i
J j
K k
L l
M m
N n
O o
P p
Q q
R r
S s
T t
U u
V v
W w
X x
Y y
Z z

© C.HICKS/96

The Thunderbird checks the Polar Bear, and breaks up the play.

"Go! Polar-Bears-Love-Ice!"
some shout, clapping their hands.

Thunderbird checks Polar Bear play breaks up he skates toward net stealing after away puck the

He skates towards the net after stealing the puck away.

He slaps the puck on goal, as a Bird tries to deflect it.

Thunderbirds

2

OK fans! "The Hockey Game Is On!", who is going to win?

Now to our next sports update:

The goalie stops the puck, guarding his net to protect it.

Polar Bears

2

Are you cheering for the Birds or the Bears, with a big grin?

Superb soccer action !

Soccer News Update:

The Dragons, in red, white and black, set an attacking position.

Knights

2

The Dragon players run forward, not looking tired.

The Soccer Game Is On !

The Knights, wearing white, blue and gold, are ready in opposition.

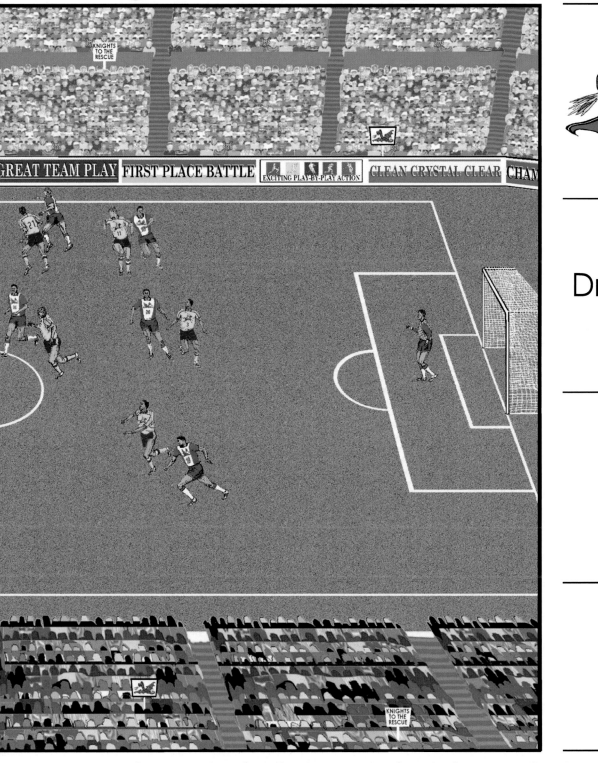

Dragons

2

The Knights sprint back to defend, playing so inspired.

The Dragons set up for a
throw-in, picking up the pace.

set

Dragons

throw-in

for

pace

picking

up

running

forward

to

win

ball

open

space

moves

A forward running to win the ball, moves to open space.

"Go! Dragons-On-Fire!", some fans cheer up in the stands.

A a
B b
C c
D d
E e
F f
G g
H h
I i
J j
K k
L l
M m
N n
O o
P p
Q q
R r
S s
T t
U u
V v
W w
X x
Y y
Z z

Every Knight finds a Dragon, to follow and guard.

"Go! Knights-Are-Heroes!", others shout, clapping their hands.

Knight every Dragon finds follow to guard the Dragons have ball fast charging hard and

For the Dragons have the ball, charging fast and hard.

The Dragon crosses the ball
with a well placed kick.

crosses

the

Dragon

ball

with

well

placed

kick

striker

his

volleys

with

head

precise

flick

His striker volleys it with
a precise head flick.

The goalkeeper lunges, as the fans watch in disbelief.

Knights

2

OK fans! "The Soccer Game Is On!", who is going to win?

Wow! What great action!

He slaps the ball away! Oooh! They cheer in a big relief!

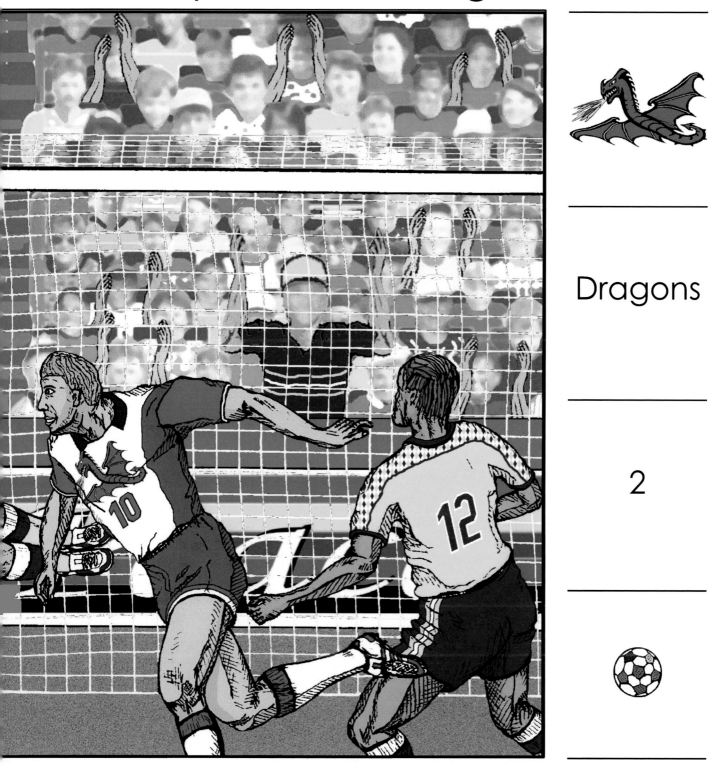

Dragons

2

Will you cheer for the Knights or the Dragons, with a big grin?

Tune in to your favorite games!

Literacy Guide Chart

Practice early reading skills using the special page format.

-The special page format is designed for children to practice key skills in their reading development.
-The story text is in black, and the alphabet letters in blue on the left, with story words in red on the right.
-This is a handy reference to practice some early reading skills, before, during or after reading the story.

4 Building Blocks Of Reading - With Suggested Reading Skills Activities

-The chart below highlights 4 specific skills that are key building blocks required to produce a new reader.
Use their current ability as a guide to focus on the appropriate skills to practice.

1
Oral Language Development

Speaking aloud and expressing ideas and thoughts builds oral language skills and provides an essential foundation for the development of reading.

Suggested Activities

- look through the story letting the child talk and tell about the pictures using their own words

- encourage, listen and actively respond to the child's own words, thoughts and ideas

-prompt for more oral discussion and detail with questions and rephrasing their words and ideas

-take turns talking about the action and what the players and fans might be feeling, thinking and saying

2
Letter and Sound Recognition

An essential pre-reading skill is recognizing all the letters (upper and lower case) of the alphabet and the sounds that they make.

Suggested Activities

- together point to each blue letter, name and make the sound of each letter in the alphabet

- explain letters have a lower case (small) symbol and upper case (big) symbol

- name a letter, the sound it makes and then have your child point to it (take turns making it a fun game)

- identify a letter and see if it can be found in a red word on the left and in the story (letters make words)

3
Building Word Vocabulary

An important reading skill development is the ability to visually identify words, to recognize the grouping of letters and to remember the word meaning.

Suggested Activities

- point to and say a red word, name each letter and their sounds that group together making each word

- point to and read a red word and then let your child find it in the story sentence (take turns making it a game)

- take turns pointing to and reading aloud each red word from the top to bottom in order

- point to a red word, have your child say the word and explain its meaning (make a sentence with the word)

4
Reading Fluency and Comprehension

Developing the ability to read words accurately and understand their meaning at the same time produces a fluent and competent reader.

Suggested Activities

- read the story together, develop a rhythm and use the rhyme to create and model a natural reading fluency

-ask questions about the action and events to check for memory and understanding

- discuss the thinking, emotions and feelings of the many players and spectators watching the game

- talk about team work, fair-play and sportsmanship, allowing your child to express their feelings and ideas

Find a good balance between working with a child's current abilities and challenging them to learn!
Support literacy development!

Sports Action Kids Books - Book 1
ISBN-978-1-7771741-6-3

sportsactionbooks@gmail.com

Copyright © Coach Craig B.Ed. 2020